The Day I Ran Away

Written by Holly L. Niner

Illustrated by Isabella Ongaro

Flash Light PRESS

For Keith, Evan, Beth, my parents, and my sisters: when I'm with you, I'm home. —HLN
To my family, teachers, and friends who support and love me. —IO

Printed in China. First Edition – April 3, 2017
Cataloging-in-Publication details are available from the Library of Congress.
ISBNs: Hardcover 9781936261895, ePDF 9781936261901,
EPUB 9781936261918, Mobipocket 9781936261925

Free printable activity pages available on our website.
Editor: Shari Dash Greenspan
Graphic Design: The Virtual Paintbrush
This book was typeset in Chaloops and ITC New Baskerville fonts. The title font is Grilled Cheese.
The illustrations were hand-sketched and digitally colored in Photoshop.
Distributed by IPG • www.ipgbook.com
Flashlight Press • 527 Empire Blvd. • Brooklyn, NY 11225 • www.FlashlightPress.com

"Guess what, Daddy."
"What?"
"Today I ran away."
"You did? Why?"

"Because my purple shirt was dirty and I had to wear a white one."

"That is serious."

"And my favorite cereal was all gone."

"Who could live in a house without Sugarific Toasted Squares?
So that's why you ran away?"

"No, there's more."

"I yelled, I WANT MY PURPLE SHIRT!
I WANT SUGARIFIC TOASTED SQUARES!"

"Oh! What did Mom say?"

"She said, 'Time out, young lady.'"

"I see. So you ran away to your room?"

"No, Silly, you can't run away to your room."
"I suppose not."
"I went to my room and made a picture for Mom."
"Good idea. A peace offering?"
"Yes. But the purple marker made me wish for my purple shirt."
"You do like purple."

"So I made myself another purple shirt."
"How did you do that?"
"Easy. I colored my white one."
"Hmm. What did Mom say?"
"She didn't like it."
"What did she do?"

"She took away my shirt and my markers,
and she shut the door.
Banished to my bedroom."
"Like a princess in a tower."

"That's when I decided to run away."
"OH! How did you escape?"

"When Mom called me for lunch I told her I was running away.
She said, 'Oh! Then I'll make this to-go,'
and she put my sandwich in a bag."
"How nice of Mom."
"Then she said she'd miss me...

...and she waved goodbye."
"Where did you go?"
"Nowhere. I remembered something."
"What did you remember?"
"I'm not allowed to cross the street!"
"That does make it hard to run away."

"Mom must have figured out my problem because she said,
'How about your pop-up tent?'"
"Mom is clever."

"So we popped up the tent,
and I ran away to the yard."

"Didn't you get hungry?"
"No. I ate my sandwich. And Mom brought me cookies."
"You must have been lonely."
"No. I had Hilda Bunny and Charlie Dog."
"Were you bored?"
"No, Daddy! I had books and toys and games and crayons!"

"No markers?"
"Not for a week."
"That seems fair.
So why did you come home?"

"Hilda Bunny and Charlie Dog got hungry.
And Mom made spaghetti and meatballs."
"Your favorite. Did you need a truck
to bring all that stuff home?"
"I didn't bring it home."
"Why not?"

"Because, Daddy!
We're going to run away again tomorrow!"
"What do Hilda Bunny and Charlie Dog say?"
"They say 'yes,'
as long as we come home
for dinner."